CHEEKY TEDDY
ON THE FARM

First published in 1980 by
Deans International Publishing
52–54 Southwark Street, London SE1 1UA
London · New York · Sydney · Toronto
Reprinted 1982, 1983, 1985, 1986
Text and illustrations Copyright © Deans International Publishing,
a division of The Hamlyn Publishing Group Limited, 1980

ISBN 0 603 00190 4

Printed in Great Britain

Cheeky Teddy is going to spend his holiday on a farm.

He is very thirsty when he arrives so the farmer's wife gives him a glass of milk.

"How are you today?" Cheeky asks
Mrs Pig and her piglets.

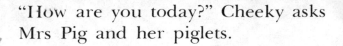

Then he goes to milk the cows.

"Have some bread," Cheeky says to the ducklings.

Next, he collects the eggs from the hens.

"Cheeky, be careful!" shouts the farmer.

Cheeky takes a ride through the countryside.

"Missed me," says Mr Fish to Cheeky.

"Is the honey ready?" asks Cheeky.

"That looks delicious," says Cheeky.